MW01124464

THE BEST RECESS EVER

To Mom
for birthing the love of reading in my spirit
and for encouraging me to soar.

— S.M.D.

To my parents,
grandparents,
and the total sum of all my friends.

— C.L.

ACKNOWLEDGEMENTS

Special thanks to Vuthy Kuon & Providence Publishing
for his consulting and their outstanding publishing services.

Also to Chris Leathers
for bringing my words to life
and capturing my vision through his insightful illustrations.

To my second grade classes,
who inspired me to pen my story for many children.
I love you all and I always will.

To my friends, relatives and everyone who supported my efforts
in a variety of ways throughout this process.

BOOK DESIGN by EXTREMEDEV.COM
Contact Charles Nguyen (832) 858-9639

Text copyright © 2004 by Stephanie Mara Dawson
Illustrations copyright © 2004 by Chris Leathers
All rights reserved.
Published by
BOOK NOOK PRODUCTIONS
PO Box 101, Richmond, Texas 77406
Publishing services provided by
Providence Publishing Services, Inc. (888) 966-3833
Printed in China
First Printing 10 9 8 7 6 5 4 3 2

Library of Congress Catalog Card Number 2004092347
The Best Recess Ever / Stephanie Mara Dawson / Chris Leathers
Summary: A young girl finds confidence and friendship through her love of reading.
ISBN 0-9748990-0-3

THE BEST RECESS EVER

author
Stephanie Mara Dawson

illustrator
Chris Leathers

producer
Vuthy Kuon

BOOK NOOK PRODUCTIONS
Houston

Stephanie is the best reader
in the second grade.

She is great at reading. Every
day she reads something new
and exciting. However, she is
lousy at making friends.

For most kids, recess is the most
exciting time of the day. For Stephanie,
however, it's the worst.

But no matter how bad her day may
seem, she always has her books.

One day at recess, Stephanie approaches
a group of girls jumping rope and asks,

"May I join?"

"No way," the girls reply.
"We don't play with bookworms.
Besides, you don't know anything
about jumping rope."

Sadly, she walks away until someone yells, "Hey, can you throw us the ball?"

"Sure!" says Stephanie. "Here you go.

May I play?"

"No way!" the boys laugh. "We're the best team in the whole school. Besides, you don't know anything about soccer."

"This is the worst recess ever," Stephanie mutters. "I'm going inside."

Inside she sees a group of kids playing computer games. "They seem interesting," Stephanie thinks. "Maybe I'll fit in there."

"Hi, everybody," Stephanie says excitedly.

"May I join?"

"Go away!" scream the computer kids. "Can't you see we're busy? Besides, you don't know anything about computers."

Disappointed and alone, Stephanie clutches her books and leaves.

When Stephanie arrives home,
she throws her books on the floor.

Tearfully she screams,
"I hate these books! They're the
reason I don't have any friends!"

"There, there dear," Stephanie's
mother says. "You can't control
what others think about you. Just
remember who you are and be
true to yourself.

Someday people will appreciate
you just for being you."

Stephanie picks up her books and goes to her room. There she reads until she falls asleep.

The next day at recess, Stephanie walks up to the girls jumping rope.

She says to them, "Did you know that in one record-breaking jump rope competition, the winner made 169 jumps in one minute?"

"Wow!" the girls exclaim. "That's amazing! Maybe you're not so boring after all. Would you like to jump rope with us?"

"Sure! I'd love to do that," Stephanie answers.

Next, she walks up to the soccer players.

"Soccer is called football in every other country except the United States," she shares, "and in India, they used to play in their bare feet!"

"Wow! We didn't know that. You sure know a lot about soccer," the boys grin. "Would you like to join us sometime?"

"Sure!" says Stephanie. "I'd love to do that."

"This is turning out to be the best recess ever!" Stephanie exclaims.

"One final destination!"

The computer lab!

There she walks up to a frustrated group of computer kids. "What's the matter?" asks Stephanie.

"Our school computers won't play the new video games we downloaded from the net," complains one of the boys.

"You probably don't have enough RAM," says Stephanie. "I read that if you close some other programs, you might free up more memory."

The boys close their music files and word processing programs, and *"Voila!"* The problem is solved.

"Gee, Stephanie! You're a genius!" they all chime in unison.

Just as she had promised,

Stephanie jumped rope with the girls.
She played soccer with the boys.
She even played video games
with the computer kids.

After school, Stephanie skips home
and greets her mom with a big smile,
happy that she had finally made friends.

"MOM," she says,
"TODAY I HAD THE BEST
RECESS EVER!"

THE END